A LETTER TO MY DAUGHTER:

A Father's Blessing to be Great

Kwabena Yamoah

Published by Kwabena Yamoah
Chicago, Illinois

Book Design: Earl Cox & Associates

ISBN 10: 1-932450-65-3
ISBN 13: 978-1-932450-65-1

Printed in the USA

DEDICATION

To my wife, Tasha, and our daughters Nariah and Anaiah, who made this book possible. To my parents and siblings for supporting me along life's journey.

To all daughters, know that you have amazing gifts, and the world can only move forward when you achieve them.

B
D E
X
Y

I am writing this letter to you my beautiful daughter, to share with you my thoughts of the amazing and the future that is you. I love you. I respect you. I pray to God for you.

These reflections accurately describe you. You are wonderfully brilliant. You are incredibly unique. You are impressively timeless.

You are not simply regular.

You are not strikingly ordinary.

You cannot be placed in or fit in a box.

However just as the sun and moon find a way, you radiate, you transcend, you transform.

Goodnight
Precious
Princess
& other stories

My daily mission in life and the reason I whisper to you every morning that the day is great, is to let you know that in a world that asks many to be the same, a world that pushes common, I give you permission to think differently, to act creatively, to love deeply.

Life will tell you don't strive. Stay the same. Achieve small things. Don't grow too much.

I tell you to extend yourself and reach further.

To look past all of your fears and walk longer.

To hold your breath and swim deeper, to elevate your thinking and fly higher.

To remove all obstacles so you may see clearer.

These things will help you find the great passion that lives inside you, and the purposes of why your destiny was created and is unfolding.

My purpose as your father is to help you bring forth your unique purposes for life.

My gift to you is to help you find your own unique gifts.

ZOO

My love for you is to help you display your own unique love to others.

Every day, you are one day closer to your purposes, to your gifts, to your loves.

I was created to help people want more for their lives, to help people become more for their families, and to help people see the greatness they have in themselves.

My gift is to write beautifully, to speak thoughtfully, to compose gracefully. My love is to show and live compassionately. To appreciate wholly, to desire strongly, to embody fully.

There is a need for me in this world, just as there is one for you.

My daughter, what are your great purposes?

What are your incredible gifts?

Who do you sincerely love? That is why I am here to guide you.

I wanted you as my child because I believe that in you resides the future of our world. I love you.

I am a Champion
I am Amazing
I am Great
I am Brilliant
I am Beautiful
I am Accountable

I am raising you to be a thinker of who you are, not what you are.

To love the whole of you, not only the parts that reflect back in the mirror.

To cherish the pieces that cannot speak for you, but because of your character, the truest inner beauty, speak to others.

That is who I am raising. The you on the inside, that makes a difference to the outside.

You are Amazing! You are Beautiful! You are Great!

If you dress up the outside, and forget what is on the inside, you are only taking care of one part, and you place restrictions around your appearance.

However, if you take the time to care for what you believe about yourself, the intensity that not only resides in you but can transform you, you have just unlocked the key for your light to shine - today, tomorrow, and forever.

Life is not easy.

Being you is not easy.

My love for you will help ease any uncertainty you will have in life as you remember my heart for you, these words to strengthen you, and you work to find and live your purposes.

My daughter, I cannot live life for you.

Though we have many shared similarities, you have a distinctive and vivid spirit, your own colorful joy, and a captivating smile. Sometimes that comes with its own unpleasant pains and disappointments.

I selfishly wish I could grasp and take away all of your distressing troubles and all your discouragement.

I would do you a great disservice if I did that for every hurt in life that you experienced.

If I did so, that is not a life for you to live, and neither is that called love from your father.

What I can do is prepare you for each day and give you this message - you have everything you need to become the greatest you this world has ever seen. Everything.

You have yourself, a mind that wants to grow, a spirit that wants to be filled and a hope to become more. These are your building blocks. I give you permission to be Great!

ABOUT THE AUTHOR

As a husband, and also a father of two beautiful daughters, Kwabena Yamoah understands that the way he displays love for each of them, and shows up to them daily, will directly influence how his daughters perceive and shape their own unique worlds. For this reason, he has written, A Letter to My Daughter: A Father's Blessing to Be Great.

Kwabena is currently pursuing a second master's degree from Northwestern University in Evanston, Illinois while also continuing his career within the federal government, where he has spent the past 12 years developing national and international programs. Originally from Ghana, West Africa, he was raised in New Jersey and currently resides in the Chicagoland area with his family.